THE PENGUIN POETS

THE PUNISHED LAND

Dennis Silk was born in 1928 in London. In 1955 he emigrated to Jerusalem, where he has lived ever since. His poetry has appeared in a number of collections published in London and Jerusalem, in a small-press book published in Massachusetts in 1964, and in many journals and reviews.

Revolution proof 10

THE PUNISHED LAND

Dennis Silk

PENGUIN BOOKS

Penguin Books Ltd, Harmondsworth,
Middlesex, England
Penguin Books, 625 Madison Avenue,
New York, New York 10022, U.S.A.
Penguin Books Australia Ltd, Ringwood,
Victoria, Australia
Penguin Books Canada Limited, 2801 John Street,
Markham, Ontario, Canada L3R 1B4
Penguin Books (N.Z.) Ltd, 182–190 Wairau Road,
Auckland 10, New Zealand

First published in the United States of America in
simultaneous hardcover and paperback editions by
The Viking Press and Penguin Books 1980

LIBRARY OF CONGRESS CATALOGING IN PUBLICATION DATA
Silk, Dennis, 1928–
   The punished land.
   I. Title.
PR9510.9.S57P8   1980   821   79–18767
ISBN   0 14 042.276 5

Printed in the United States of America by
The Book Press, Brattleboro, Vermont
Set in CRT Caslon

Some of these poems first appeared (some in different form) in various
periodicals and anthologies, including *Ariel, Encounter, Harper's, Midstream,
The New York Times Book Review, P.E.N. Israel 1974, Explorations,
A Face of Stone, Retrievements,* and *Springtime 3.*

FOR HAROLD SCHIMMEL

Contents

I. From *A Face of Stone* (1964)

God's-Eye View   3
The Bankside Pastoral   4
The Butterfly   5
Lines for a Friend   6
Rimbaud in Childhood   7
Lessons   8
The Mirror   9
An End to It   9
Revolution   10
Sleeper   10
Letter from an Angel   11
Aspidistra   12
Yiddish Song   12
Guide to Jerusalem   13
In the Everlasting   16
Passive Between Hills   17

Thorns   18
Gog and Magog   19
Couplets   20
Midsummer   20
Truant   23
The Wadi   24
Conversation   25
The King   26

II. The Constitutional
The Constitutional   29
This Beetle   30
The Jacket   30
Waiting   31
Tenses   32
Beginning   32
Under the Weather   33
Cut-Out   34

III. Stud Farm
After Maurice Scève   37
His Boy, His Cream, His Pest   38
Letter from Isaac   39
The Painter's Story   40

IV. Night-Jargon
The Nursing Fingers of London   43
The Park   44
The Brother   44
Returning   45
Graftings   47
Wake   51
Morsels   52

V. Laissez-Passer

    Prologue   55

    Channel   56

    Laissez-Passer   57

    The Confidence Man   58

    England   59

VI. The Punished Land

    Watch Out!   63

    The Scratch   64

    Basic Training   65

    The Young Lieutenant   66

    Sleeping Gun-Crew   67

    Meal   68

    From This Hilltop   68

    Soldier Silk   69

    The Soldier Blockades Suez   71

    Like One Pushed Down   72

    Ahmed   73

    Forlorn Hope   74

    Epilogue for Schweik   74

    Epilogue   75

    Ark   76

    Patrol   77

VII. The Blue Poems

    Induction   81

    Holiday   82

    Climate   82

    The Two of the Two of Them   83

VIII. Nest

    The Open Strings   87

Taxi Station   88
Girl Travelling   88
The Gamesters of Jaffa   89
The Bored Table Lamp   90
Kef   90
Captain Kidd   90
Wanderings   91
Visiting   91
The Daring Gardener   92
The House   93
Beau Monde   94

IX. Silence, and Stealth of Dayes
Hospital   97
Bug   97
Traffic   98
Here and There   99
Silence, and Stealth of Dayes   100
Scarab   103
Housekeeping   104
A Dream of Fair Women   105
Names   106
Frontier   106
M   107

X. Stopping Place
Portrait Coin   111
Sky-Picture   112
Weekday   113
Stopping Place   114

XI. Songs for a Theatre
The Blind Broom-Man and the Queen   117

The Double Rows Back   118
Masowka's Song   119
Songs for a Thing-Theatre   120
Performance   123
Sherlock Holmes   123
Eating Days   124
Theatre Manager   125

XII. Guide to Jerusalem (Second Edition)
     I Dreamt I Was Flying   129
     Shapes   130
     For the Ancestor   132
     About the Double   133
     Silly Fool   134
     Fancy-Free   135
     Ein Karem   136
     Guide to Jerusalem (Second Edition) 138
     In the Street   142
     Tuna   142
     Candidate   143
     The Capital   145
     Exercises   147
     Temple Builders   148
     Here Is the Washing Place   149
     The Troubles of Tryphon   152
     Mătronita   153
     Loom   154

Notes   155

I. *From*
A Face of Stone (1964)

for Alice Arbel

❧ GOD'S-EYE VIEW

It is a god's-eye view: watch a scythe working
round the yellow grass, and watch a partridge watching
from its nest in grass, watch how that partridge
flies at the scyther's face, dares to decoy him
from its harboured eggs, watch how that scyther
scoops up those eggs in his tattered sweaty hat,
and thinks of his lucky supper.
                                        Now the partridge
need not fly out at a scythe, can safely fly
to some other Sussex field. And its eggs plump
a poor farm labourer, and all is well,
the eyes brighten of a god, and all is well,
perfect, adjusted, from a god's-eye view.

◀ THE BANKSIDE PASTORAL

for David Shahar

A farmer who had been expropriated
tired of the deathless seed, he lay all night
in the marble stockyard of a bank, and heard
the specie breeding. Oh how quiet it was
where no flies tormented, only the lovesick
smile on the face of silver, and the crooning
of copper coming together. A decent man,
he was ashamed his armpits smelt so vile
among the marble. In his farmstead he stank
of necessity he now shook off.
Watching the specie breeding apace, he wondered
how it was he and his wife had never known
love was so clean and easy.
Now he was like an old and shriven monk
guarding the bank's portals only after a lifetime
of dissipation among worldly things.

THE BUTTERFLY

from the Czech of Pavel Friedmann

He was the last. Truly the last.
Such yellowness was bitter and blinding
like the sun's tear shattered on stone.
That was his true colour.
And how easily he climbed and how high.
Certainly, climbing, he wanted
to kiss the last of my world.

I have been here seven weeks.
Ghettoized.
Who loved me have found me,
daisies call to me,
and the branches also of the white chestnut in the yard.
But I haven't seen a butterfly here.
That last one was the last one.
There are no butterflies, here, in the ghetto.

◆ LINES FOR A FRIEND

Y.C.

The pallid wine your clever lips drank
distastefully has sobered you.
At the last you drank yourself under
the laden table you had praised so long.
Now you are pruned to a new shape,
but I recall you seated, still
rambling in your Irish way.
Prophetess at that table, order
red wine, and laugh
till wine has its good body again.
Don't find so much
silence in a long-stemmed glass.

RIMBAUD IN CHILDHOOD

Today he scowls, and would revise the sky, but his paint box
has run out of colours. The clogs of the peasants clump up and
down, and this pleases him better than the Latin hexameters
he now prepares for his mother. He scowls again, thinking of
his fingers between her fingers—those ten bitter instruments
of a twisted justice. Justice will also be revised but that comes
later.

1

What does a child drink?
Doctrine and milk of his mother's breast.
What does a child learn?
The island of his name and body
against the increasing strangeness of the world.
Fetched down by her maternal dream,
he looks up at his mother
and studies the riddle she has not solved herself.

2

Sent out from the meal to wash his hands,
he plays with continents of soap bubbles,
and comes back clean and dark.
What does he eat?
Bread pellets of rebellion,
and, seasoned by the table talk,
salt beef cut up fine.

3

Terrible to eat
prepared food with the dead.
They rise to conduct him
among the living trees.
Terrible to watch the pendulum
and not to know why the whole clock strikes.

THE MIRROR

The wrong face staring back from the right mirror,
assessing like an executioner
the unmirrored self—in that daemonic shock
you stand there with a rope around your neck
which the executioner tightens to an end
more imageless than mirrors understand.

AN END TO IT

A fine woman gave me her cloak. It fitted easily, much too
easily. Later, when I knocked at the one true door, the Muse's
door, no one answered. Now I sit quite still and, whenever I
have an itch to open my mouth, there's a grinding of teeth in
the soul.

Expounder of the faith of others, patron of new art forms,
professor of the nasal scream, I forgive you everything but
your volubility.

There is the bluebottle buzzing again. Kill it! Now the room is
silent.

⊗ REVOLUTION

A bitch once a day on her dark constitutional
hurries her master down streets, and the earth round the sun
bitch, master, and streets and everyone.
No one loiters of the large or the small procession,
all praise the bitch's litter and the new lunation,
and rejoice at the ephemerid and the perennial.
Yet revolving still his own revolution,
while dossing in doorways of the employable,
here is a shambling and sleepy and thoughtful one,
who with his wicked fingers shuts out the working sun.

⊗ SLEEPER

He has this new uncomfortable disdain,
thin arms stretched out, lids shut upon a pain
even the pouncing light cannot explain.

A beggar contemplating suicide
married dream's shadow-lady but he cried
because day found no substance in his bride.

Yet with this sleeper all that he has dreamt
leaves him no coward but dangerously intent
to force on beggars what his dream has meant.

⊛ LETTER FROM AN ANGEL

I write long letters to your shining face:
Why did you thrust me down and down your stair?
Jacob thought Bethel a visionary place;
I hated, and hate still, his holy air.

Can Jacob have a freehold in his God?
I sneered in Heaven, and then you sent me down
to call him to you with a cryptic nod
and build him a new nation with a frown.

Later I wrestled with him through the night;
I wounded him and left him in his tent.
Nothing could please him but the infinite;
Claiming you wrenched his thigh, he was content.

And all the Rachels and the Leahs, all
the concubines, the Josephs and the corn,
and clinging vines upon the prosperous wall,
proved that your thrust-down angel was forlorn.

They could have found your face, Jerusalem
forsaken, and the local ways they kept.
But when I saw what you would make of them,
I lay upon the ground and manlike wept.

ASPIDISTRA

On the sill squats an angel, aspidistra of the sleeper. Caterpillars explore his green and innocent veins; they munch an angelic salad.

In dream the sleeper fingers the trembling sap. Gentler than ambition it swells. Aha aha say the eased lungs of the sleeper taking in air in a new way.

YIDDISH SONG

Roustabouts, laugh.
A waiter works with bottles
to make you what you should be.
Honeycake for the pauper,
a drumstick for your darling,
the breast and wing of a chicken
and the wishbone are yours.
Tear the patch from the eye of the blind
and watch them wink.

Glutton, look up
from your plateful of carp
thinking of its black pond.
Carelessly smooth out
the cloth that covers the hole you know.
Brandy, burn away
the whine in the throat of the pauper.

GUIDE TO JERUSALEM

Don't live in a frontier town. It's governed by the
bad will of two countries.

—Pinchas of Koretz to his son

1

Jerusalem is a limestone cracked
by destitution, it is a beggar rattling
his tray for money or Messiah.
Here the past walks with a religious stoop at twilight,
talking to itself overmuch.
And the bawling prophets are all dead;
the pious in their conventicles
are not consumed by any rapid fire
fetched down by the former travelling angels.
No bush burns in streets narrow as doctrine.

A stranger here, poking around town,
observes the only holy visitor,
in border slums the five-o'clock light
shining like a ghost on the washing of the poor.

2

NO-MAN'S-LAND

A house stands in the sinister land,
its top floor a slanting staircase
accepted as such by aspiring weeds,
and outer walls by some personal will
of stucco and of braced stone
married as never Jerusalem.

13

Married, but living in barrenness.
Not even a stupid hen
to lay thriftless eggs here, not
an amorous cat.
Weather is the tenant now.

3
for Shalom Cohen

"Heat in gay colours," and Herzl riding
from Jaffa to Jerusalem.
"These three tracts must be bought. Make a note.
These three tracts must be bought."
But the beggarly Jews
of the Eternal and moribund city depress.
"Pond ducks when the wild ducks fly by."
He lodges in Mamilla Street,
courted or hated, a giant
or a jumped-up Jew, observes
local holiness that needs
some interpreter to sweep away its dust.

Then von Bülow waits, and the Kaiser,
and he dares to talk of Palestine; they consult the map
of the dry wells.
From the Kaiser's encampment he drives back
to a town of paupers and ghosts.
How tall he looks in Jerusalem
in the *khamsin* time, driving back.
Scared of his new blaze,
the town becomes a somnambulist by midday,
winces at sunlight and pulls down the blinds.

Just think how this corpse rolled all the way from London to Jerusalem, along a concealed but commodious tunnel, fed at stations on his way by repentant Adam, a mourning Shekhinah, and Elijah's ravens. The silly thing didn't know he'd snuffed it. For three days before his death he'd mumbled: "Not on this day be Thy judgment, O Lord, not on this day be Thy judgment, O Lord." He rolled the entire way in this prayer-cocoon. When they told him, at Jerusalem, he was dead, his chrysalis died of shock.

5

Doubtless at Delphi the priests cheated
the Pythia of her words, and sold them
to Persia if it paid enough.
She should have lived among atheists.

No place so noisome with flies
as a streaming altar, and in this town
the small guard the tombs of the great.

6

A hemmed-in dependency, I find
sun, water, stone have other names
in this exile's town.
And I have no name
for the aridity or the peace of Jehovah.
A ghost looking for a body,
I enjoy a small enclave of the sun.

1

In the everlasting the groom and his bride
scoop out whole hives of honey.
It is the memorable taste on my tongue.
In the everlasting the generous outgoings of honey
hurt the loins of the staring cherubs.
In the everlasting.

The poverty of my loins screams.
Flat cherub faces stare through glass
and laugh.
The companions on their bed in the everlasting
shiver in the zone of honey.

2

The enormous sprawl of them, absorbed in the honeypot,
these linked and laughing ones, two heads on one pillow
in the double-backed joy of God.
This diamond being cuts through envious dreams
of anyone married in law only.
Those climbing toward it are trees canted
by the steep and holy gradient.
Those climbing toward it
are stumblers on a killing scree.
These linked and laughing ones
keep the honey for themselves.

PASSIVE BETWEEN HILLS

1

Passive between hills, among
everything heavy and mineral,
the blood dares to hate its motion,
the quick loops or the hovering,
rants at its light and tedious master,
confers with the ponderable stone.
Foreign between hills, it finds
what is not stone sunk deep as stone:
the bluethorn with shrewd spikes of white
embarks on no enfeebling journey.

2

Free in the prison of these hills
(the blood says to its light master),
I would be a sullen stone
and you that harp the wind plays lightly;
I would be a scowling stone
and you that kite the wind plays lightly;
I would be a spiteful stone
and you that blood the dogs lick up.

THORNS

1

They grew spiky and tense
and struck out everywhere,
struck and scratched and grew;
the scratch of life in them
scared me the most.
Such dry and angry souls
between limestone hills
beat the traveller back.

2

It was not the mineral silence scared me
between limestone hills.
The life of my feet did not scare me
between limestone hills.
It was the mineral sap of the thorns,
it was dry souls working a language out,
making in limestone a mouth, scared me
and beat the traveller back.

GOG AND MAGOG

1

Chalky plants in dried-up watercourses
reminded him of himself.
He thought of his weakness as he looked at the rock,
and of an entrance to rock,
to lie there in the receptive veins,
a mineral king with a shut mouth.
Not to founder among foothills
and lesser names,
he went into
Gog and Magog, that rocky mountain.

2

To go a long way into nothing
among the unlucky veins of this rock,
and to lie there like a stunned king.
To enrich the rock with one's blood,
to stare long
at one's history in the rock.
To look at the rock-doves
and suffer,
to envy even the sap of plants.

❧ COUPLETS

Because she thinks extremes are better so,
she says to fire, Be fire, to snow, Be snow.

She pulls the climber down the loved abyss
and pacifies him with a limestone kiss.

She watches from a window of the Ark
her frightened children drowning in the dark.

❧ MIDSUMMER

for Allen Grossman

1

The frightening enterprise, midsummer, closes.
What did it do in eternity?
It came from nowhere, was planted in somewhere,
and gives off heat.

From such quietness it set out
to become the loud cicada.
The dry light of the olive tree
cannot even suggest the shy first light.
The eucalyptus, the long pod of the carob,
whatever the price they're alive
and know the open secret.
Intricate, terrible,
nowhere becomes somewhere.

2

Nowhere was a house of quiet light; it was a house
where no one comes and goes, and all are together.
We who sat there in the gentle shock of light
agreed not to talk, we thought no seed
of the carob and the long summer of the cacti.
Because we lolled in the house of light
a tall virgin whipped us out
and down, and through a corridor, to be born
in a world moving toward midsummer.

3

From soft loam, cruel clay,
rejoicing and trapped forms grew.
Fields throbbed like a beast's flanks;
we heard it, always in earshot,
then it was our own heart, beating vigorously.
In midsummer the clay hardened to terror;
we heard a eucalyptus breathing
and late wrinkled fruit fell.
How can she weep and be so calm,
this virgin whose milk curdles in the world?

4

This happy exile stood
among the stones of the field.
She watched the quick doves.
They flew and were discovered
by rejoicing eddies of the air, they breathed
delicate breaths, they circled above water,
in flight not deathward-inclined.

This happy exile stood
among the stones of the field,
and was sorry and glad.
Who from her house leaned out
and drove the young doves downward
with the breath of her being,
at the window of her house will laugh
and clap her hands to see
the remembering doves return
from their long journey.

5

There was no one else in the field.
Someone with an averted face
had averted her face,
and walked steadily along no field path
toward nowhere, from which she had just come.

⟨ TRUANT

You rise to stay.

You are not south or north or east or west;
you violently rest.
"Such waywardness is death,"
crows the weathercock forever out of breath.
Forgive his indirection,
his sense of being always out of true.
All direction must begin in you.

THE WADI

All the flies of that amazing summer
buzzed round him where he was. He laughed to see
the last outhouse buildings die away
in desert dust. The wadi waited
with a troubling whiteness reminding him
of a woman's face, and all approaches
in the late afternoon beckoning on
to her mad precipice and listening pools.

She was the rockface talking: when he looked up
from his trembling hold, he saw her doves
circling above vertigo; when he looked down
her pools were waiting for the sound of him.
Lucid in his foothold, he worked back
to the sarcastic edge that scowled at him
because he had returned, and there he lay
in the hush of that amazing summer,
having seen her doves and every metaphor.

☙ CONVERSATION

"Do you think I would do it for the pleasure only?
No, no, Mr. Silk, they flogged me till I agreed.
Basically I am a very frightened man.
When they told me hell was divided
into two factions, the floggers and the flogged,
even then I never would have agreed."
"Then why?"
                "This was why.
Hell's clocks move backward at the pace of the world's,
ticking away they measure out what's lost.
Watched by indifferent clock faces
the reconnoitering damned revisit their lives,
till the clocks fail, and even for you will fail,
jarred by the crisis of a calmest treason.
At my thirty-second year all clock hands failed.
Now that all hands failed, it was
timeless prolongation of the whip."
"And so you agreed?"
                "As others may
who follow the clock hands even now, Mr. Silk."

✎ THE KING

1

The king's sinking into himself
on his throne, and every attendant
flunky's bundled away, his fingers thrust
once into jewels tingle only with themselves.
He's coping with kingship now the throne room
smalls to the size of a darkening king,
and the queen and a whole garden of bird-cries
dissolve outside the throne-room door.
"Forgive me," he begged his exiled queen
and the five petitioners
sent away unanswered.
"I'm going into my swordless self
to look for the security of kingship."

2

A discarded queen trying the scentless blossom
and the listless five petitioners wait
till the king in triumph ride by.
Blossom will be scentless until
the king's nostrils discover blossom,
the palms of the petitioners will not shine with silver,
the body of the queen will not shine,
till the king in triumph ride by.

II.
The Constitutional

THE CONSTITUTIONAL

for the archpoet César Vallejo

There is one in the half-light works.
I hear you clearly, César Vallejo.
In the half-light you whisper
my new address.

Entering,
I wear the dun-coloured coat of poverty.
Like the beetle I found
this simple colour on a long road.

Curbs watching my feet all the way
and at the end a dead man
sits at the table slicing bread.
He makes me a place
in the half-light.

I sent ahead
my feet in their hope of the honest labourer.
What you slice
crams the shadow in me.
Yes, my impossible shadow
leans on your cloth.

In suburbs ample without you,
considering your traces in the pit,
it has been Benjamin walking toward
his brother.

THIS BEETLE

This beetle
cannot be christened again because
it has been christened by the dusty skin of air.
In a place ashy as chalk pits it is diminished,
it is no longer honourable, no longer a beetle,
it is Joseph in a chalk pit
looking at the bad brothers above.
In his simple shirt he must answer all the brothers.

THE JACKET

I will lie in the corner of my room,
a cast-off jacket,
and long for the discipline of a hanger.
There'll be encounters with chairs,
a stone floor like the sea.

Strange the eye of verse registers this.
In some glassy sense I am not here
yet I already lie here
buttonless and entire.

✎ WAITING

I opened the linen cupboard
and found him counting every stitch of his shroud.
And in the loft
the dying news was read to my brother.
My elder twin was waiting and flying,
a guillotined feather on the night-road.

Sitting in the pantry I wasn't done
with compote and jams.
I told him to wait
and gave him a pastry-cook
conical hat tall as a heaven.

Here is the starched hat
and the apron of my brother.
In his new uniform
he grapples with me.
Here is the stitch of longing
in the shroud of my brother.

TENSES

You have lived in three
and trisected life so cleverly fits
this partition-grave which cannot be called common.
It is a limb here and a limb there,
the forehead cannot think back to one,
the word
is hot and unstitched.

BEGINNING

Under the heartbeat a phantom
saying It is not I who stir the sugar.

You drink tea in a café with too many hats
too many coats on coatracks
unwrap the little lump
and stir what clouds me.

And there's a paper bag in your house
from which that same stuff pours onto the floor
till it's the soil you walk on
candy for the party
where you shoot and laugh.

Then I stick up my spectral hands
for your trigger works well.

Child of malice,
sugar-heart, are you beginning?

UNDER THE WEATHER

1

On that long walk from the wayside station, the weather itself, the sullen Levant, squeezed into my travelling bag. And it crouched, a shrewd devil.

Yes, you had kept house at the heart of the plantation. *Do you know my poets?* A tea-cosy kept the poets warm. But I thought your slightly démodé dresses hung from a tough palm tree.

A cake trolley scared me. You wheeled it against me like cannon. Heart, I said to myself, you're under the weather. A doily won't save us now.

2

Men are changed by the things they carry. A sheet of glass, and a man is a glazier. That's undeniable.

Here's the packet-man tying himself up. He never once addressed himself to the muse of string.

Or the shoe-shine boy who never got out of the polish. He's in disarray. What does he do when he looks into the shine?

A hat brim lifted a man. What will become of me?

3

Muse of paper, of the rouge and comb of an unhurried toilet, muse of unflurried conversation, ransom us in a cluttered room.

1

Your head won't need its hat anymore. It lies here oddly intact without its trunk. Was it some Judith who cut it off? Your arms like dolphins fly about their business. Your feet stand in their pumps at the Coroner's. Someone has made a cut-out of all your parts.

2

Won't you join the dance? I won't, you say, No I can't. I don't have a breath long enough. I've the left lung of a suicide, it refuses to breathe in. What's that musician trying to do? My left leg keeps Greenwich time, my right's gone to sleep in New York. Is that a wedding march he's trying to strike up? But my ring finger's divorced its hand. My hat's an affront to this street. Merely tooth marries air. Greedy-guts, saying *All right*. (But it is not right not to publish these banns.)

3

A whistle blows. Someone is directing the traffic. For the wedding, in the next street, of dismembered man. Careful, you say, gingerly. I can scarcely pull myself together, scarcely stand up. With a somewhat sheepish smile you ransack your memory. Send your leg down looking for your ankle. A scouting party to look for your wrist. Eight then ten fingers. Ditto toes. Two or so eyes. (They are not glass.) You're kitted out. Tear ducts and memory. You put your best foot forward. You're a man of parts.

III.
Stud Farm

❦ AFTER MAURICE SCÈVE

1

*Absorbed in her toilet, white daybreak
was dabbing on the rose and the gold.* . . .
Will that do?
                    My dismembered understanding,
returned under drawn curtains to me
from the too much of too many things,
infused me against dying.
                                    But you,
and only you, can explain
the perplexing pavement of each day.
You're the incorruptible myrrh
against gruesome worms eating me.

2

Hecate, you'll fool me, I'll loiter,
live-dead, a hundred years, among shades;
you'll turn heaven's key on me, Diana
(yes, you who bait this trap or planet);
you'll drug, or allow, my double pain,
mother of the submerged dots there.
    But as Luna injected in my veins,
moon of thought among the afterbirths,
I name you—first last always—
a foreign call among sterile thought.

⬬ HIS BOY, HIS CREAM, HIS PEST

REVISITING BERRYMAN

In the ward a drinker
and a cureless doctor.

Can there be recovery
for Henry?

"No no," say the ward walls,
"simply, at intervals,

a poultice of dream-song
to soften ward-wrong,

phenobarbital
and a sharpened pencil."

Short-breathed dream-songs wait
on Henry's long-breathed fate.

❧ LETTER FROM ISAAC

FROM ISAAC BABEL, IN RUSSIA, TO HIS
MOTHER, IN FRANCE

Behind the big Russian stove
the breathing of calves warms me.
They're carried to our cottage through snow.
(Our Molodenovo
pokes out of a mountain
of the snowed-up moon.)
Taking the air,
so that's what a hand looks like, I say.

Venerable and nervous Mama,
I'll consider all this drift
just a while.
Touching a muse,
I laugh on the stud farm.

Loneliness you squeeze from your tubes
talks Italian. "Il Capitano,
the Cap'n" . . . You paint him Groucho moustaches
so no one will think he's scared.

Sloping, this hill
deviates from the studio where you paint courage.
A vine lives in fright here, asthmatic plant
breathing when it can.
"It's all right, all right."
Your wife nurses
its irregular gulps of air
against the sky.

From the vine
she extends her arms over this whole hill
where she and you live
and your dog Bam
on a lonely farm.

IV.
Night-Jargon

◆ THE NURSING FINGERS
OF LONDON

I look at the greeners through the window,
the little parents sent out from Vilna and Dvinsk
even the knout could not kill but London did,
nursing and gently wringing dry.

◀ THE PARK

Wheeling our shadow on
with the delegation of other shadows, Alas!
for the metropolitan
concord in loss.
Our son
lies in the pram
of London.
Alas for the crybaby
in the great park.
We have given him the password: Dennis
to open the gate.
(Dennis shuts.)
Alas for us
when concord has the smoothness of zero.

◀ THE BROTHER

for Yehuda Amichai

I loop the loop
to catch myself,
in the aspidistra-room, Paddington.

And it's not projection.
I am myself looping
in London,
hat and mac, bulky.
Watts don't melt me
as I do my ℓ for the sister.

◈ RETURNING

1

From expansiveness and hurry
to contraction in a ship's cabin.
That, and dining-room heat,
induce an extraordinary torpor.
I do not remember the weeping Arabs yesterday;
told, today, of their harbour goodbyes,
I could only stare at Mike in amazement.
Our cabin lies immediately over the propeller,
or so it seems, and it tires me
to work with the propeller all night.
We're sailing toward London, that heavy foreign sound,
in the *Adana,* from Haifa:
ornate Turkish salons and halls
like a dream of international finance,
talk about money across glass tables.

2

The slightly doped passengers
look strange to the working crew.
They defend themselves behind Turkish,
at stations crouch and laugh,
one polishes a window while his friend talks.
Even the purser defends himself from us,
changes money, but true language is in his fingers,
below deck no doubt talks also.
As for me, I've the dictionary of the propeller.

3

We drink wine with the dancer of forty-five
waiting to be discarded for all her power.
She is coarsened and perhaps true.
A beautiful Arab in a cheap European suit
joins us — colt's first day out,
he's got a job in Paris.
These careless transients, back in the cabin I think,
haven't been polished to a town-shine.

4

And it is London underneath in the propeller,
that's what I fear.
Once past Lyons the heavy weather begins,
the fog of sacrifice.
I say, Mother, forgive
blood connections, the floundering, the body's drag, water,
and to my sister,
What are you waiting for, so noble and foolish,
in the shoe-shine city?

1

a
Father and mother,
I'll go down to the cellar to find you
where the deserters crouch,
packed into barrels, salt herrings
of the old dispensation.
We share a patrimony of shadows—
nothing royal—of substanceless demons.
This gruel we eat together
is the best I can offer.
A slow spooning-out, mother,
a tired eating, father.

b
Your son studies
freedom large as the half-moon on his fingernail.
Fingers work and die.
A half-moon white and flourishing in the cellar,
swallowed by demons.
Not to be affable with them.
As the cellar steps mount
my words to arrive,
father and mother,
in a little clearing,
a half-moon, unassailable.

c
One struck out
along field paths to the frightened villages.

One fed all day in town.
One, a moon-swallower, devoured, disgorged
all night in the cellar.
Petals of the moon, flaking, assembled,
a whole moon-flower, a family to be picked and die.

2

I fatten the substanceless with a sigh.
I drop my coins into that empty money box
till it clinks.
Bellyful of the human, and the watery marrow rejoiced.
In the conduits of the city, the veins of the citizen,
a thin devil-transfusion.
Who's that under the hat brim?
Under that brim a weak smile for the human.
Soon not weak, fortified by the human.
Ach, such graftings very often occur,
graftings, and occasions.

Like that girl who stared back
at greed staring through a window.
As it is, a wrong one went to her wedding.
He enjoyed his seignorial rights every night.
Substanceless weight creased her pillow.

Listening to devil-conversation in the air,
carcasses of souls
buried where the vacuum shapes itself to a smile.
Yourself could go out into the electric light
and be eerie.
Nothing to do there, manikin,

but talk to the midge-cloud of the electric demons,
and even on Mars nothing to do.
Nothing to stanch the substanceless wound
but your own bleeding.

3

After such demon-swathes through the field,
we are in the sun's shed where the gleaned are piled
high as mangolds.
Food for the sun's funeral, the humble and gleaned
carelessly pile up.
Carts brought back
pulp of voices.

4

They take the whole field.
You can watch them, a long line of cotton pickers
finding their way,
famished and plump with rebuttals
for all you say.

Whose name are you?
Through the eye of the needle
as the poor through heaven
wander, but work.

5

Your travelling expression usurped
by demon-blankness,
how the fat wheels laugh.

Your private devil sits on a milestone and laughs
at you through the window.
Devil of sums and wheels,
he jogs beside you and laughs.
He teaches your forehead
the discomposure of heaven.

The binding place has been carted away.
You look at an idiot landscape
covered with doodles.
By the devil of the wheels bluffed,
you sharpened your pencil and the train came.
You were good at sums,
you multiplied the square root of nothing to get there.
Pleased by the steam whistle,
how the fat wheels laugh.

6

From where I lie
I can't judge the teeth of your horses.
They take the horizon.
But my face among the stooks watches you, carter.

Tied-up blood of the stooks,
father and mother,
before the wheels come, cry
against the wickedness of the carter.

1
D.S.

Severity
of the wake over, it is Asia
I with you share, the play
of son and mother.
Night-windows
of the enormous rooming house
open dark as is white
wake-milk of you.
At the *d* of death
my lips are frightened
but they make for you
their night-jargon.

2
J.S.

The street map stales
you read so carefully.

"I am not,"
you say to London,
"in Kensington
or Willesden
or any
street name,
not comfortable
by a coal fire October

or November,
not in any
room once rented."

You are vague
and follow your meander home.

◄◙► MORSELS

for Jenny

I have of mother
a hand glass I would like
to defend myself from because
a soul must not loiter and I
must be strong in my day or strongly vague
as one looks in morsels for a deadline.

V.
Laissez-Passer

❧ PROLOGUE

for Varda

Do they eat there?
Palestine is a poorhouse, I thought,
or a place where you go to lie down.
Can you walk, there?
Is it like London, does it have windows?

Palestine calls you out,
father-tree answered.
Toes won't know where to go,
you'll have so many.

Don't loiter in English.
Take your hat and your head. Go!

1

To shake off English sleep at Calais!
I laughed in the pier glass.
French glass laughed back.

On the ferry my countrymen
frightened me with little lumps
and spoons, a blackballing
cold club of saucer holders.

Rigor mortis
of a trouser leg, dead lace
at a wrist . . . the twitchy survivor
makes his wardrobe-song.

2

The Englishwomen hang like clouds
or the clouds are Englishwomen.
The barometer cringes
and suffers their pale woman's burden.

I've spoken to
the Hyperboreans, the giants under ice.
Go away, they said.
A vapid north of talk
condensed, and got us.
Go away quickly.

LAISSEZ-PASSER

for Dan Tsalka

The domestic weepers
can have my carpet slippers
and with my London pastimes
I leave them at the Customs.
*It would be suicide
with you,* says the blonde bride.

It is the last of England.
Small talk. Dwarfish talk.
I never asked your hand.
Language grows and smiles
at the lazy sea miles.

Water does not stale.
I lean over the rail
and read with persistence
the map, mother of distance.

✒ THE CONFIDENCE MAN

for Arieh Sachs

With his hat and his hands, why it must be the possible new author.

He's old to be such a young man, thinks Mrs. H. the publisher. His eyes look tired, he must be a map reader. Tell me about your travels, Mr. T.

Mr. T. does his Rimbaud. A dog, and patience. A full purse, sometimes. The breath of goodbye.

It's a long time? Mrs. H. ventures dreamily.

Yet here I am eating bonbons in Sloane Square.

But how *do* you make out over there, Mr. T.? Do you have a chair in poetry?

A chair! I can hardly manage a stool, Mrs. H.

Then how do you make a living, Mr. T.?

I catch money-birds from the air, Mrs. H. Can you hear them? *Tweet-tweet.* Yes, I too belong to the English songbook.

ENGLAND

It is odd to talk there
yet they do talk
as a pebble of the watercourse
that left it for another.

It is hard to be pebbly
till tongue talks
as it should to a friend.

I began as an Englishman,
in a small way,
and I found the big blue
at Marseilles.

VI.
The Punished Land

for Isaac Rosenberg 1890–1918

Argument: These poems are about a land too beautiful for its inhabitants. So they punished it (or rather her) with a general ill will—Jewish, Christian, Muslim. She survives, parcelled out, and in hiding.

Sometimes she hits back. Perhaps she's also a punishing land.

She's called Palestine because it's her best name. It's not the Palestine of the Fatah, or the Greater Israel of the irredentists.

. . . red clay in a chronic battlefield.
—Noah Stern, *Stopgap Letter,* translated by Harold Schimmel

❧ WATCH OUT!

Jumping down I found Palestine
mined for kicks.
Several soldier-jokers called out in khaki.
Watch out, my boots said,
watch out when the laces fly
through holes of convenience.
Weather is otherwise.
Time to go home, second toe said.

Second toe, champion beauty,
don't go off with the Palestine map.

Watch out, my beauty, the mines said.
I knew it was my country I felt so various,
felt I was geography.
The mines said
you too, you too, are a crack of a man.

THE SCRATCH

Bang bang.
Palestine tommy guns again.
On lips, through loops, the hate.
Over the counter I bought
a bandolier and a water bottle,
under the sun, in a slouch hat, made it
on the kilómetres-hike.
                              But the scratch!
The Jerusalem scratch festered.
The pus on my little finger grew
a whitening township in the big country.

Pus, little river
of kindness, now we are the nephew
of the big country.
Here is our milestone-mother
and our grandmother.
Remember her kindly
and she'll talk to us nicely.
Poor little scratch, she'll say.
Poor wounded Palestine, we'll say.

❧ BASIC TRAINING

I've phantasmal army boots,
and a khaki Bible,
and a heart of Hebrew.
"We're in Asia, *habibi.*"
A melon-stand road hopes for the capital.

I hitch otherwise.
English in a German beer garden,
talking Kant at Benares,
and in Cairo Volapuk,
I am ambitious everywhere.
Zrīfin the camp names itself.

THE YOUNG LIEUTENANT

KITTED OUT
(ZRĬFIN)

Webbing attaches itself
and camp earth.
Lots of colour at the butcher.
Mother-ochre.

You're the lieutenant
of a colour that worries you.

THE PLACE

Kitted out,
running down staircases in twos,
pushing down slopes toward an end.
Never a single one but twenty,
at the side, behind, gesticulating.

You should have thought of this before
the young lieutenant unfolds his war map.
"Here is the place," he says, "here."

COMMANDER

Upper lip
can't control the map of Palestine.
Nether lip
slouches from the battlefield.
Whose mouth
dominates the soldiers then?

The young lieu—
in lieu
of a lip who's the tenant?

❦ SLEEPING GUN-CREW

We worked for the Father up there,
pushing the daylight weight of his gun
round the half circle of our patience.
Father, poor Father, we say,
at Lights Out we scoop out
a foxhole in the Mother.
(Father, poor Father, till washed
by such tears his wife allows.)

Adonai, poor Adonai,
in stretcher-sleep our brain grows,
our meat is your woe,
our language in earth,
we grow tall on the tubers
of the Mother of cordite,
Ashtoreth of the ammunition boxes.

❧ MEAL

Palestine earth
in my palm
eats the life line.

❧ FROM THIS HILLTOP

From this hilltop,
apart but with us the general peers
into the smoke where we are.
He would like to learn the plan of battle
and help us.

Worry-clouds.
Hill not elevated,
plain not smooth.

Someone
planned the battle
and willed the tall field of thistles
we cannot get through to make sense of.

SOLDIER SILK

1

Binoculars carry the dream-burden.
He scans from Hierusalem
a Cairo of cries and flags,
Soldier Silk scans
Nasser, smile of a false carnation
(into these glasses, also).
Nasser flips through
the whole dream-file,
claims he's
the moon's boss,
blackmails Mother Isis,
in Cairo, munching
from the accidental feedbag.

2

Binoculars carry the dream-burden.
He scans Isis from Hierusalem,
Soldier Silk travels through glass up
the Lady-canals.
She phosphor-signals,
the despairing crescent fish, scaly
the third of her
under glass.

3

In Jericho she
landscapes Luna Park.

Here are the real snorting horses.
A few boy-soldiers
survive the roundabout.
This is the poinciana Lady
awarding surprising petals to dwarves.
They thank her under Jericho lava.
(The command car
lurches ahead.)

4

Piled-up Pharaohs
molest Isis.
Tools and nuts
kept the convoy going,
petrol, and the real
scorpion in the binoculars.
The pass
humped its back and let you down.
All the hairpin
drivers are going home in a hurry.

5

In Cairo Isis
smiles on her assassins,
moon-men and lovers,
through Presidential suites looking for Nasser.
These demoniacs find her
the little diminished tube of him.
Black pusher the moon
tries him between her fingers
for three puffs.

Jerusalem, June 1967

THE SOLDIER
BLOCKADES SUEZ

He dips three toes in the Great Bitter Lake,
two in the Little Bitter Lake,
adjusting his binoculars spans
Kantara.

Spots Nasser the big ship
and his herd of ships
unmilked and lowing.
They low. He laughs.
Look, he says, *at the*
cowlike dead ships.

❧ LIKE ONE PUSHED DOWN

After the throne of queenship is lowered from heaven
a seated woman begins to walk.
After the tiara is lowered from heaven
a bareheaded woman stumbles.
In tall circuit of a small room
she arrives at furniture.
Saying good-bye to the Great Above,
she conforms to the laws of a cupboard.
She wears cupboard commode drawer shelf.

She arrives at wardrobe.
She wears the sizes of this world.

A salesman unrolls
his bale of cloth a street long.

Please roll up that bale,
Ishtar.

AHMED

Tiny he was shaken out of the big map.

British-Turk. Boom-boom.
He was two, then,
the fall guy.
Arab-Jew. Boom-boom.
Sixty, now.

Shall we curl up and sleep, now,
in the big map of the Trucial States?

FORLORN HOPE

Soldiers arrive at a valley between two towns. And scattered over a meadow there, a peaceful battery of bedsteads and cupboards, tables and chairs. Opening drawers, the young lieutenant sorts out family papers. A mortarman finds a Penelope, a chair still rocking.

EPILOGUE FOR SCHWEIK

Now boots walk in their sleep,
Schweik, rescue my little
and my big toe from cramp.
We'll loll in the capital.

And it's not that colour-sergeant who called out
but the young men as we advanced,
rearwardly, sweet Schweik, from the front.

EPILOGUE

A shoehorn could ease my thought
of laced life.
Big left toe wants out.

But I've this black boot
to go round,
shiny as a town,
to salute,
a colour-sergeant to say my prayers to,
till boot-acreage thins,
and the toe of a thought flies out the window,
a dead soldier, a real thought
doing its kilometres,
the small saint of a toe
the battalions stub ignorantly.

☞ ARK

"Hazy weather, Mr. Noah." Visibility
nil, and in the Ark bits.

The animals went in toe by toe,
eye by eye, joint by joint,
spine
loitered for suicide.

Bits, its,
itsy-bitsy bits,
o my   o we   o they.

Instead of an eye a finger
stared through a porthole at this flood
and didn't report back.

Who'll repair a hernia
through which intelligence spills?

Will Adam
who named each beast in his park
and pondered

the three parts of his finger to touch with,
his hand to fondle and to steer,

confer his north on Noah to grope through
this herd of strayed bits?

September 1973–March 1974

PATROL

in memory of Evyatar Cohen

Conical-shaped mountains and a queer culvert
after the tents where you started.
A grumpy track with streams running against it,
heaped mountains like a camp of tents
till Berekh of the white gate.

We have a household
where colour never runs,
salt in its cellar always crisp.
You drive toward
the household of that mother for everlasting.

Your mother
burdens the tear-bottle that cannot hold you
and, turning back,
you'd talk to her from a tender chair.

Yet it's the deep furniture, drawers
and cupboards of the other place you open.

VII.
The Blue Poems

INDUCTION

Travelling from your oval forehead
he's neither one nor two.
His identity disk talks about him,
sweetens his neck, tells him he's
one more incurable hoping for vastness,
drilled numbers. It hangs
insultingly, and will not die.

So your discounted animal's
kitted out.
Please undo this button.
Pretty word Abyss
where we go.

HOLIDAY

Now you are in Greece and listen
to Delphi and the other tongues. I hope
they'll talk limestone to your frittering heart,
and decisive sibyl-stone,
the weight of woman in all that place,
talk the child away.
                            Who else could be mentor
to the lingering child, the Grecian butterfly?

CLIMATE

Heavy heavy damp
in whitest paper. London.
                            Mother
of you who shouldn't walk
in the macintosh they put on
there, to be poor and armed.

Blue and new your nursery soul walks
in this light. I call you the Greek girl
because you're limpid.

✿ THE TWO OF THE TWO OF THEM

The join of daylight man and woman
is rarely common. Under the coverlet lie
the friendly ghosts of two but two sit
and eat with knife the accomplice and fork
the table-lie, the salt-lie, the egg-lie.

He is an account keeper,
she off and blue somewhere,
unhoused side-glance hoping for a corner,
a table leg to rest at.

A hand
from back there, a tongue
travelling no distance, might help
subtraction to be generous.
                            From their banquet
under the coverlet, cannot
the kissing cousins help, lean
toward family,
the poor eaters of daylight?

VIII.
Nest

I know where there's a bird nest builded down on the ground.
                                        —Charlie Patton

⚜ THE OPEN STRINGS

She's visited by handsomest males
before they lose their courting plumage.
Her sky-blue notes scare.

Why, she must be Apollo's daughter.

ᴓ TAXI STATION

Tattooed an earlier name
as hers on his, a hand
I touch for goodbye at the taxi,
his name in my time.

ᴓ GIRL TRAVELLING

Odd you ask me how my left hand is
as though my health's there. We stare
after such politeness. *It's all right,* I say,
but my left hand is very bad. The charge you give me
then go off as always, odd girl,
with your uncommitted hand and your tattooed hand
into the traffic.
                How is my left hand
and right, the toes that attack me
because I am with them so seldom,
and because I mistake me, no I am not all there,
nor with you among gnats of traffic that would bite you
because you are there.
                How is your hand
and your left hand and your right hand
and that danger carefully you shield
on the way back and from time to time touch
and garner carefully in your palm?

THE GAMESTERS OF JAFFA

Backgammon players of Jaffa, you shake so many plurals a mind can scarcely guard its singular. Yet your little cubes cannot find their way down the meander of a side street. A more winding man's needed for the deep play.

He works through the spiral of a seashell to get there. Here's someone turning gamester eyes on him. All Books of the Dead print the candidate soul's interrogation—it's got a laissez-passer at best. Here, strictness sits at her private table.

THE BORED
TABLE LAMP

The bored table lamp
found its watts.

Dice are cubed
when you roll them.

KEF

I want to be with you
when *kef* spreads.

The chemical wedding
is you and me
in a cigarette.

CAPTAIN KIDD

Captain Kidd
is you
and a wild harbour.
You laugh,
comedian,
in a sanguine scarf,
pirate
boarding pale boats.

WANDERINGS

1

Is your house Number Sixteen still? I thought it was the square root of nothing. Shooting lights, as I lean against the wall, warn me not to try this too often.

2

They look quite homely in the sky, these fireballs. If you like a home of fire. My friend does. Watchful at the sill, she laughs.

Her door's funny. If it opens, I go out in vapours. If it doesn't, I go out in vapours. Either way, I don't see much of her.

VISITING

You've arranged tables and chairs
of your wild will
in new waves.

Wading out they say
it was nice in the old pond.

Saucers and talkers.
Tea cakes dabble.

You irrigate
my photograph of you.

Someone should make a calendar of waves.
I think *sea* is a nice word, don't you?

THE DARING GARDENER

You plant the Mary Ann tree
who are not a simple Ann
or Mary.
It is not an offence in heaven
when smoke of its green
touches blue.

Neighbours rifle
Mary Ann because she
is generous, they
unneighbourly.

They coax the thin world
into a cylinder
and watch the coils they do not follow.
They can not smoke
the plant of sky.

◄ THE HOUSE

"Make a picture of it." I did
as she said.

A palm
above uneducated grass.
That cut sun of an opened fan
scrutinising through an upstairs window.

I fixed it. She smiled,
the left hand of God, at my effort.

The fan
of fair women
grudges to disclose
a face and will stint it
at the first betrayal.

I walk my memory, I exercise it.

Many and teasing
smile particular.

I retrieve her among many
not easily scattered,
a hive of women.

It is vague and fixed.

❧ BEAU MONDE

Suddenly one discovers you have family.

A sister (though some say of a foster father,
not a first father),
and her father,
and then someone married to him.

Why you're flecked all over with family.

Sometimes in your iris
sky and you falter toward each other
till a modish man
walks into the blue.

I do not know to decline you:
I see you
blue not blueish,
wounded by blue
you cannot parry.

In sky
the beau monde of receding fathers,
each defers to a bluer one back there,
bluer and bluer as it defers
to an earlier one climbing
through the mad hole blue dropped down from.

IX.
Silence, and Stealth
of Dayes

❦ HOSPITAL

I died almost: now I'm the bluejay's feather
undustbinned and keeping a good height
above smoke of smoke dingying the valley
and rising from stacks where others lie.

❦ BUG

1

A door opens and the bug gets in
and lies in the wound. Jack-
in-the-corner. Aboriginal
among aboriginals but older,
he goes with the furniture of the hospital.
Tired wood of the electrocardiograph,
yellow screen for private occasions,
your locker or little home, they're
all made for the bug.

2

He cleans out your wound.
Can you bereave him?

Every facet
of bug-crystal shows through
to there but here is a sweetmeat,
candy-heart, here is a window

to long through and a valley
through glass but the bug
says goodbye because
you never had the mileage.

TRAFFIC

In an Opel or Ford,
and as ever reticent, Raymond
and Gershon, the well-known dead,
nod from their car and drive through.

HERE AND THERE

Four rings of the lamp
throw that strongly ethereal shadow
from which they hang.
It is the twofold muse
of the clumsy corridor.

Hospital
is heavy.

Muse muse! cries the short-memoried medicine bottle
trying out the name of the mother
but corking itself against her.
Scales want to weigh her but get surly
with the shadow that undermines them.

Only the bedstead maintains its sorties
into the shadow,
enjoys an airy name there,
honest climbs back into its iron legs here.

Queer for the intern to watch a ferry-bed
that does not know whether to be metal or angel
and would like to be neither or both.

⊠ SILENCE, AND STEALTH OF DAYES

Silence, and stealth of dayes! 'tis now
    Since thou art gone,
Twelve hundred houres, and not a brow
    But Clouds hang on.
             —Henry Vaughan

1

I take the rain-path back to my house
through bushes no saltier than myself,
in a cloud of all souls.
                Death-flecks.
The town looks pretty at night.
I can watch the walking dots from this hill
of bad counsel.
It's a silly kind of rise.
The squashed look of a hat
or if glass looks scratchy—
some bug
wants me to be its golem.

2

Gold bug of good counsel,
your transparent side
bares overmuch heaven.
You'll hocus me into a trapezium
and I'll freeze there.

Through the morgue of a thousand
that yield their yellow party-frocks
the bug throbs and conducts.
I think he wants me into *maybe*.

100

A broken chair, maybe, a cracked cup,
glued in heaven.
Town-crumbs.

It is a willing furniture.

He's so geometrical.
One two three one two three
he say to his women.
(Mathematicians
are terrible seducers.)
He wants a thousand gold bugs
to lie with.

Aurora
who tilted toward heaven
Sèraphita
cozened into pure being.
All the posthumous names.

He asks the mechanical doll Olympia
to dance with him.

3

It's like wiping a cloud
from my brow.
Now they are nameless drops
in the grey universal
and now a milky hand pulls me up into this cloud
or I pull down a milky hand
and tardy and greedy.

All this is bug-business.

4

Do you think you're going into the crystal state?

Once you've climbed the great staircase
a curtain of dots parts to let you through.
In the great ballroom, Olympia,
dots many dots
court your spine of an odalisque.

This dance floor has need of a set-square.

The Plato-bug lied,
Sèraphita.
                    Aurora.

Crystalline women,
I can not shape your name in this place.

SCARAB

In the wound to lay
your egg of real life.

Pharaoh's muse.

Or is it usual
                    bug-colour
you nurse?

A monk
        digs a cell
in this room
                    translates
his dirt or pokes it
into a corner.

❰ HOUSEKEEPING

This girl handles
the dots from there (pensive,
inside herself found them).
                       Dots and
daughters of dots.

Household.

Only not to fawn
on the flux,
she opens
a window of conjecture and stares through.

A DREAM OF FAIR WOMEN

A cloud, a ship of fools,
wail to disembark. White fools.
This cloud's paramours cry to climb
by their hair back but they have no hair,
extend in troth hands
but they have no hands.
These no-bodies do his will there.

Dots
in white where the crystal
smile was.

A tongue takes a talk
while it can.

A duchess of nothing
is dangerous and a countess
of cloud.

A starer
at this ship of fools
dares to make of cloud a word,
in the meantime
a substantial word.

I look up at the shape-changing
spooky town
of a parallelogram god,
a dot god,
the pure slurrer with a mouth
to undo any vowel or consonant.
I cannot hang your photo
on his Bauhaus wall.

NAMES

1

I nursed a typewriter
(Adler *circa* 1916)
till it became a young pen.

2

IN MEMORIAM ADLER

The window was open
for him to refute
terminal cancer.
A small egg grew
in the big hospital.

FRONTIER

You are
men not dots? did not
ebb in a jelly-panic? are
the friends of your name?

We see
you are trying to make us a spine.

We must be careful
about the household of dots.
The flux sends its spies down.

M

When I help you into the M coat,
even though you "don't like
being ladylike,"
I extract my fingers
from the N stuff.

Cloakroom hooks
sing in a wrong key
to the attendants of a freezing music.

I want to sit under a hat rack
and think.

Town-hats
and dots for heads
and N
hovering.

X.
Stopping Place

⬥ PORTRAIT COIN

I study
young lucidity under a lamp.
Valuable coin of 1953,
you'll not blur.

The lamp goes out and we are in the street again.

This portraitist has done even the laugh.

Now we make our odd passage
down the street that has not turned out well,
you turn me over in my mind many times,
and I must take out the street map to get it right
though it is a complex of grievances.

I call this coin the "unforgettable"
for it has been disposed of in argument many times,
I circle and circle this inscription many times,
and the horn of plenty,
and the laugh that is withholding a look

in a small inept street
where we deepen the town-blur
with your head that is not tunable.

SKY-PICTURE

1

And my religion
is a girl-woman. That can't be.

Her room's dowdy
without her, she's needed
for real light is cut off.
That can't be.

She's here already
in yellow frock of consolation.
I'm her son.

And she
keeps house
and sky.

2

The only land
is a housekeeping cloud.

Recently I promoted myself to a cloud.

It lifts me
from motherland, I arrange the tale
of our meeting, *she*
is the tale's gift.
Clouds are white liars.

It is not at all bulky up here
nor amusing as Congreve.

The sky-picture
is interesting
but it is not a floor
or a woman
of altitude.

And I am not the priest
of a blue of blue.
You are skied here,
skied here,
cloud-key.

WEEKDAY

Morning boots wade.

But you, and only you, can explain
the perplexing pavement of each day.
You can not. Then who? Can a gap explain
to subverted leather and to wool
the pale colour of its authority?

Gingerly, again, the enlisted toe
in the boot. Goodbye, Sunday.

STOPPING PLACE

To be a street Arab
saying wrong words
in the rain!
In the stopping place
I'd not be maladroit,
we could dry out there.

No, not a whitewashed room.
                          Wallpaper
colours that do not bang
into each other,
towels, and a shoe brush
of character.

XI.
Songs for a Theatre

THE BLIND BROOM-MAN AND THE QUEEN

(*from* Parade)

Queen: They fill me in with cement and night.
The blind broom-man is my heart's delight.

Broom-Man: They fill you in with mortar and brick
but I tap toward you with my broomstick.

Queen: I feel so heavy out of my nest.
Lag-goose flies east, lag-goose flies west.

Broom-Man: Here is a rowboat built for a queen.
It has the best oars I never have seen.

I have swept in my pan your dust and fright.
(*Rows off with her, using his brooms as oars*)

Queen: The blind broom-man is my heart's delight.

THE DOUBLE ROWS BACK

(*from* The Double)

I am rowing and rowing.
The sea is this darkness.
Will a child ever get back?
Darkness of father and mother,
darkness of this birthday.
How hard I row, I surprise even myself,
I am every finger of me holding this oar.
Soon I will be over, it will be over,
the other lip of that sea whispers.

🐟 MASOWKA'S SONG

(from The Doll's Journey. Masowka, a doll from the
Japanese Bunraku theatre, travels to the death
camps.)

All the mothers are in the carriage.
It is so stuffy and they ask,
When will we reach the railhead?
At each wayside halt they ask,
Why don't you sing, Masowka?

At Lemberg the sadness,
at Cracow the pain,
can't scare my song.
At Lublin I wear
my sash of proportion.
The lonely train whistle
scaring the women
can't scare my song.

The lonely train whistle
longs for the railhead
and I for the mothers.
I crane my neck
to look for the mothers.
Looking back they say,
Why don't you sing, Masowka?

SONGS FOR A THING-THEATRE

(*from* Mr. Charles' Chair)

1

a

In this theatre
I talk to a chair
or a sly old corner.
I play you my belt
Albert.

I hazard
Daisy?
and clothe my little finger
in her.
Gertrude or *James* are you
what hide and laugh?

I dice
in dark.

b

     And unwind
this cotton-reel.
Yes, I'm the comedian
of a needle and rummage
in the drawer of small actors.

Here's my *C* thimble
and all the keyboard of sundries
I play.

The commode
coughs and is musical.

Of a ripped one
I cannot find a single stitch
yet sew steadily.

2

THE NOTIONS MAN

From a fifth-floor window
to throw down bobbins of thread
and buttons with ample holes
and wear a serious look
as the town fights for his gift.

Nice collection of buttons, Mr. Charles.

To do well by the hat
and not to forget the boot
or toe or the mouse
and to milk the chair
and Gregory the whole room.

Things appreciate the working man.

3

WHEN WE DEAD AWAKEN

Early A.M.
Clubbable chairs anywhere.
This dimmer on a sofa
subtle or brazen.
No one and everyone.
Dew lies on early theatre.

4

RETRIEVEMENT
for Micky

I follow all the cues
in the light-book of memory.

You were the priestess
of ridiculous things—
Captain Boot
Field Marshal Mouse—
comedians we sent out
to tease the pompous capital.

Yet you were serious
in all your entrances and exits.

I seat you
over the *Charles* things
of our expired play.

◀ PERFORMANCE

The god came down into the boot
and fumed there,
took Irving strides
across the boards of the bedroom,
went out,
tough old actor-manager,
into
a glass of water and was calm.

Smalled
into a shiny button.

The eye
of the god-button,
inquisitive, inquisitorial
among bored things (us),
that eye
was the travelling sleepless being
in the sleep-room of things.

◀ SHERLOCK HOLMES

Sometimes a bloodspeck in the long pursuit;
sometimes, in the evening, a boot.

EATING DAYS

We love our spoon but it
does not work now
and the tilt
of the salt-cellar is not for us.

Filleted
day, and smoky,
beef of days,
are we a finger-
fork?

Do we sprawl in the stadium?

Here is a napkin
we don't fold because
it is too fine to follow.

∾ THEATRE MANAGER

Climbing your stair,
I have the hundred thoughts of the playwright
and am a long way from the quiet table
of poetry.

I find a crumpled man
and had prepared for an enemy.
Affable, you walk me around
the patio of your small thoughts.
Is that the sky there?
Considerations stain your brow.

You are the factor of a small dream.

The children of the greenroom,
your actors,
denatured by a pointless repertoire,
and spangled, jump through the hoop of many plays.

They are lawless and vague.

Yes, it is hard to be the captain of a ship
and its purser.

Here is the stairwell of vertigo
for it dizzies to climb so high
toward the plebeian.

XII.
Guide to Jerusalem
(Second Edition)

I DREAMT I WAS FLYING

1

There are houses that share the vertigo of doves. These are the cowards, they are rightly called, Houses. There are lintels that say to the dove, Where you sweat I fly.

2

A Fool and a Magus met one afternoon on a tightrope stretched above Jerusalem. The police station was below, and the Russian Church, and the hospital. The Magus, fearing the Fool was about to say something, tried him with one word to forestall many. There was this one word, *Fall*, on that tightness of rope. He was sorry for the word he'd been forced to pronounce, and even as the Fool fell the Magus wanted to retrieve him. The altitude laughed at the absurdity of that want.

❧ SHAPES

in memory of Avner Motzkin

"Here was a horrible wolf [*indicating a point in decaying plaster*], yes, you see its nostrils. And this is a beautiful man, you can see his head and shoulders. And I saw the descendants of the apes, much nicer than humans today. And this is a very obvious Venus de Milo. And here's her pregnant mother. I'd lie in the room for hours, learning the shapes. My wife was very jealous. Of course I didn't tell her but she knew it was to do with the room. I'd see Chinamen with moustaches and, playing with swords, Eiric the Red, Hitlers. And then there were two emotions. When I was afraid I ran: when I hated them I fought them."

"And now, Avner, if you scraped off the plaster, would you still see the visions?"

"Yes, of course, because once seen I can always see them. The Arabs knew about irregular walls. They weren't afraid of the shapes. Now my friend Avi has been having visions since he was seventeen, but he didn't realise the Chinese stay on the wall. It's dangerous to learn the shapes unless you know they stay there. Avi propositioned Dorit. When she refused, he said: 'Then let me just stay under your bed and watch you painting.' Madness is when you believe you're mad and start hurting others.

"It must be difficult for you to listen and understand all this, the result of two years' contemplating. Now I've too many practical problems but I paint a painting a day and see the visions in the paper. A painting a day keeps the doctor away."

"If I steal some of what you say, Avner, is that all right?"

"Oh, I'll be flattered, everything is for God."

FOR THE ANCESTOR

There was this inscription in Arabic for the ancestor. Not your ancestor, intruder, I heard someone say.

That's not true, I'm wet-nursed by all the dead.

There was this inscription in Arabic for the ancestor. If I'd looked a long time I couldn't have found it. And I'd been looking a long time.

The old house waited for the new tiles. Somewhere among them was the inscription. It was hiding or hidden, they were stacked in the garden.

The tiles oppressed me with their look of the newborn, very new, not written on at all, with their foreheads of willing conscripts in some war they were already fighting.

On the battlefield, under the battlefield, there was this inscription in Arabic for the ancestor. It pleased me to think of him as the only innocent. Maybe he'd vexed the innocent, had been the bramble for their sleeve. But now he was the only innocent.

There was this inscription in Arabic for the ancestor. The tiles waited like angry decimals, or foolish virgins for the bridegroom. He'd lost himself, laughing, he'd been lost, pushed aside by impatient virgins. They'd never be courted, that was certain.

✎ ABOUT THE DOUBLE

1

The Double invented the trapeze, his likeness the safety net.

The Archbishop of Doubles rowed around Jerusalem with his friends.

He was in disguise, he was dressed in his Double.

The Double is the important cousin.

The Double lopes up at dusk.

There are two towns.

2

Last seen at Damascus Gate, smiling goodbye to his likeness tracking him through a telescope.

What did he live on? Stray puffs of a tramp's cigarette, essential vertigo, the befuddlement of his likeness.

Who was his tailor? Someone's needles and pins came back black from that experience.

He sat there in his stolen shoes, plotting against Jerusalem. Only a Double, or a dead man, could wear them. They weren't the shoes of the sleepwalking town. Two pairs of shoes wore down at the heels in two different towns.

133

I wish I could tell you more about the Double. He's the missing finger which makes ten a tragic chorus. They look histrionic and silly. Try again, dunce.

❦ SILLY FOOL

Jerusalem, my dears!
Why, it could be Algiers.

Iris, an English fool
at finishing school,

ambles through the *souk*
with the wrong grammar book,

will conjugate, decline
Picturesque Palestine,

wear an Arab frock
at the Dome of the Rock,

and ask what she can't,
and would, of the Levant.

FANCY-FREE

Barkhash, mosquito-dainty,
though not solitary,
wait for Lights Out.
Frankish blood
they sip and sip
because they are Saracen.
These insurgents
are rubbed out on white walls.
It is the big
or the small.
If *barkhash* don't trouble you,
in a way they're not there.

EIN KAREM

for Harold and Varda, for Ivan and Aviva

Cow-parsley with your eternal
fly from England,
don't sadden this hillside.
There is a herb here against you.
Green and medicinal and unbottled,
it saves the morning tea of friends.
(Uncrushable sage, we need you.)

A mauve-black button
at the heart of parsley,
a housefly,
and in his field
a London schoolboy
saddens.
He wears a peaked school cap,
probably,
in that locked field.

Waves of thought as of terraces
unlock me.
My voice here,
hoarseness assuaged,
enlaces
London and here.

Bowls of thought
in a donkey tethered
through fore and hind leg,
and a terrace above, the master
burns rubbish.

Voice, battlefield, holiday.

The fly that came from England,
and settled here,
buzzes in this holiday poem.

Cancel that buzz
on this hillside
where the herb grows
that assuages
among friends.

Passover, 1978

GUIDE TO JERUSALEM (SECOND EDITION)

I have heard 'em say, sir, they read hard Hebrew books
backwards; may be you begin to read at the wrong end.
—William Congreve

1

DOME OF THE ROCK

A fantasia maybe, guns going off,
fireworks too, Mohammed's scorched feet
at an altitude above the town
rise from the powder and matches.
Even the wicked Turkish walls laugh
at old musketry, charred laughter
at an old climber.
               The catherine wheel
alone rotates to heaven.
Your hand tries deeper
that bagful of Maria Theresas,
bounty of this narrowness of streets.

2

JOHN BULL IN MAKHANE YEHUDA

Sir Bull, you're back.
Among cheap sweets, propped dolls
lolling toward their wedding,
and all the hanging creatures
rendered down and sold here,
you're the High Commissioner
of a rolled-up umbrella,
enjoying a mandate

of cough drops.
Ask the proprietor
for a new name.

3

He's just a marijuana boy
delaying in Jerusalem.
The sibyl daily telegrams him: Come.
In saffron and yogi sandals
sacramental.
On marijuana
sailing toward and receding from Jerusalem.

4

BAZAAR TUNE

He prefers leisure to work.
He's an agèd Young Turk.

5

THE Y.M.H.A. JERUSALEM

Are there lessons at the Y.M.H.A.—
you can name for them the English beasts—
English lessons for the Hebrew children?

Grammar pays the grocer
certainly, the light queerly
finds your wicked hand on the board.

It starts from the left,
this hand, like all wicked intentions,

all hearts, does not know how an elephant
runs in Hebrew.
It belongs to the other side
with their flags and forts.

6

Tank traps or ghost traps
in Musrara.
                    Mandelbaum
his gate opens.
                    Influx,
Mamilla of the drying flesh.
Souls?—Washing hung up,
shirtsleeves of the ghost flung out,
by pegs trapped.

Influx?—And more.
Shantytown, you're the proprietor.

7

I am frightened of mouths
accidentally primed that kill.
It is the town-chatter that finally frightens.
Mouths of smallshot
primed kill.

8
SCALE MODEL

I observe a model of the Second Temple
expounded by an old religious woman.
She walks among the ample measurements,
Jerusalem big as a box.

It is a toy lying in a box.
Now it is limp as a gollywog
but could lash out like a jack-in-the-box.

9

Scary city cobbled with thought,
you coded your name
in the doodle of a cul-de-sac
for the easy daylight reader
to trip in the cracks.
I read it translated
on a moon-map, or striking matches.

❧ IN THE STREET

I don't know you in the street but once
you held my thing in your hand, my essential thing.

❧ TUNA

The two porters, priests of the fish, sawed hard
to get through salt and ice at the victim.
Dead tuna eye all over town.

Great eye of God in the porch
where the Russian Church defends a mystery,
not a sweet voice
stopped the sawing.

This dead man at the pharmacist, he's
skyward a little already in the photograph.

I cannot hear you for the rhythmic
sawing of the great fish.

◄█ CANDIDATE

Down there, in the lower reaches of the Muslim world, sat reading his exam-mark Nusri Atrid the beetle. Then he bought himself a revolver.

He killed a king or so, ate an ice at Groppi's, pushed off to sisterly Syria. He junketed around a bit, the wallpaper was disagreeable at Damascus (though there a gold bug climbed the wall of hashish).

He addressed it the first stanza of a poem.

> *Pharaoh-bug,*
> *exhaust a gold pain and lay*
> *the egg of my real life.*

He had his coat buttons sewn on at Baghdad, wrote a second stanza in Kuwait.

> *Royal bug* [it began],
> *you come at me like an assassin*
> *full of courage.*

He mislaid a stanza in Bahrein.

In Aden he played billiards a lot. He had his shoes soled in Oman, heeled in Isfahan, yet never tilted an inch. He wrote the last stanza in a train, looking out through its window at newly seeded Georgia.

> *Grow down to a grub. Finish.*

After all, it was only a stinky Levant egg, he told himself. All garlic and hope.

By now his buttons didn't match, they looked like a Common Market of buttons. They troubled Georgia.

❧ THE CAPITAL

1

In the speech hall I sit and think
of the lost tribe of syllables

reru and *lalem* holes in Hebrew

The speakers
have thought themselves out of their buttons
their speech is lacy and free

With all that pneuma overcoats
billow and hats
laru and *relem* in the pensive air

2

Laureates
sauntered through a strict parlour.

I'll knead a
pumpernickel against them, yes sing
coarse bread.

Pumper-
nickel, Pumper-
nickel, Pumper-
nickel the golden.

Flatulent capital.

3

I've forgotten any petty name
except the wise king of partial judgment
overreading his canticles.

He spooks around
and hopes for the little sister
of a lost cadence.

〓 EXERCISES

1

Six days in their weird conical hats
(as in Piero)
and with horns they told the walls, *Brace yourselves*
to undo yourselves.
The seventh day seven times,
next a great shout,
a slice of sound and a block of sound,
and seven complete six.

Music coiled back,
nasty in the spiral of the ear
of Jericho.

2

And with vile and holy acoustics
they made the sea dry
and musicians walked over.
Unmusical horsemen followed
and hooves sank down an octave in that sea
and though you went down two octaves
you could not find those horsemen or that music.

⬣ TEMPLE BUILDERS

One-winged angels with hods gather moodily before the temple builders. *Just a cubit more,* says Hiram. *Windows of light,* says Solomon.

Who can control this work gang of unruly djinns? Hovering between moon and set-square, they're so flighty you must play them like kites.

Twilight twists its queer fingers, halfway between this and that.

Hiram and Solomon have enough on their hands. They dare to channel the long thought from there, to shape it under their mild hats. All the foreign wives have gone to sleep. Measure bruises the forehead.

HERE IS THE WASHING PLACE

1
PETRA HOTEL

They wash well.

Yes, pilgrims know
H_2O

who are children
of Jordan.

Taps work for them!
think the mem-

sahib so dry
she could die

and her Baghdad
man who did.

2
ARMENIAN WASHING OF THE FEET

The ankle's happy, and the little collective of the toes.
The foot is very glad to be in communion with the hand.

3
HOSTELRY
for Harold Schimmel

Refectory queen,
rose of Sharon,

serviceable
at table

in a tumbler.
A waiter

pours her for them.
The pilgrim

drinks the small town

of the mother
of water

drinks her first son
second son

beneath mirrors
holding cutlery
and plates of white.

4

Difficult
for the Elohim woman
in Jordan shallows.

5

Because there is no river in Jerusalem
do you think you are a mountain learning to swim?

You must swim past all the faces
and laugh at flint.
The only bruising quarry is stone
wanting to be water.
The dead course of the wall knows you.
Smile back at the handkerchiefs, swim
round the Turk-like wall of this town.
The dry wave.

THE TROUBLES OF TRYPHON

BIRTH

With his living glass of water, Mr. Tryphon's ejected from the sea. A glass? A tumbler. He does handstands without losing a drop.

ARRIVAL

Mr. T.'s arrived at the outer suburbs. He waters the town-tomb. Thirsty dead lick up his charity. Yet his scales are unrefreshed. Landlubber. He cranes back at the sea, bland and copious, from which he came.

GRAMMAR

Is the sea in the glass? Or the glass looted from the sea? Mr. T. says the sea is in the glass. But his soul leaks.

He can't pretend it's charity. It's simply his bad aim. Mr. T.'s deflected a glass of water.

A Dead Sea voice. Starting off well, ambushed in the larynx, dead in the room.

Ah! If he could water these houses without turning his back on the sea. The sea turns its back on the thief.

✺ MĂTRONITA

1

The mountain is wild with men,
has her pilgrims, her blood,
where her blueflower
launches you into the valley, laughs.
Claims her lieutenant
shot under her wall,
khaki in the wadi grass,
combs the hair of her suicide
in his crumbly halfway house.

2

Surface tranquillity in the stone
makes it talk so high
yet it fears
underground waters of the Lady.
She calls
Petra in Jerusalem to her.

3

The Scandinavians, the hitchhikers,
their haversacks from the sea,
taste petrified town in their mouth.
Walls of May have a hot taste.
The riverine consider a mystery.

Listen to one under stone
blond, and dark, do not hear.
She alone unfolds the town plan,
sculling away on water.

❧ LOOM

A man from Hebron
played on his loom how to get out of Dennis.

Clack clack—dreamy train journey—strands
submitting to the penetration of the weft.
Cotton-rhythm   journey-rhythm
the dunams of God.

Fruit of this workshop in the *souk*
gets fingered and sold, I ate it when it was growing,
Dennis Dennis a man of this century,
grammarian
of a skull-clutter of sound.

✎ NOTES

The Butterfly. Translated, with the help of friends, from a Hebrew version of the Czech original. The poem was written in Theresienstadt. Pavel Friedmann was killed in Auschwitz at the age of twenty-one.

Guide to Jerusalem. In 1898 Theodor Herzl visited Palestine and had several audiences with the Kaiser, a pilgrim at the time. Quoted lines and phrases are from Herzl's *Diaries.*

Letter from Isaac. The first three lines, and the ninth, are taken from Babel's letters.

The Young Lieutenant. "Lieutenant" to be pronounced, English fashion, "lĕftenant."

Sleeping Gun-Crew. ". . . the half-circle of our patience": the gun had a traverse of 180 degrees. "Ashtoreth"—Hebrew style: Ashtórit.

Soldier Silk is the younger brother of Schweik. He hasn't seen most of the service registered here. ". . . accidental feed-bag": the windfall of U.S. aid. "Luna Park": a tiny Luna Park in Jericho after the June War of 1967. ". . . crescent-fish": this is what the moon looked like, seen through the strong lens of a Japanese telescope the first night of the war.

Ark. "Hazy weather, Master Noah." The one surviving phrase from an old puppet play, *The Creation of the World.*

Patrol. The last consonant in "Berekh" has the sound of *ch* in *loch.*

The Open Strings. John Jay Chapman said on his deathbed: "The mute, the mute. I want to play on the open strings."

155

Portrait Coin develops an image from Borges's *The Zahir.*

The Troubles of Tryphon. "Tryphon": a mythical figure who visits Jerusalem in 1837.

Mătronita. Moshe de Leon's muse in *The Zohar.* The mountain is Mount Zion.

Loom. "dunam": a unit of land measure used in Israel, equal to 1000 square meters or about ¼ acre.